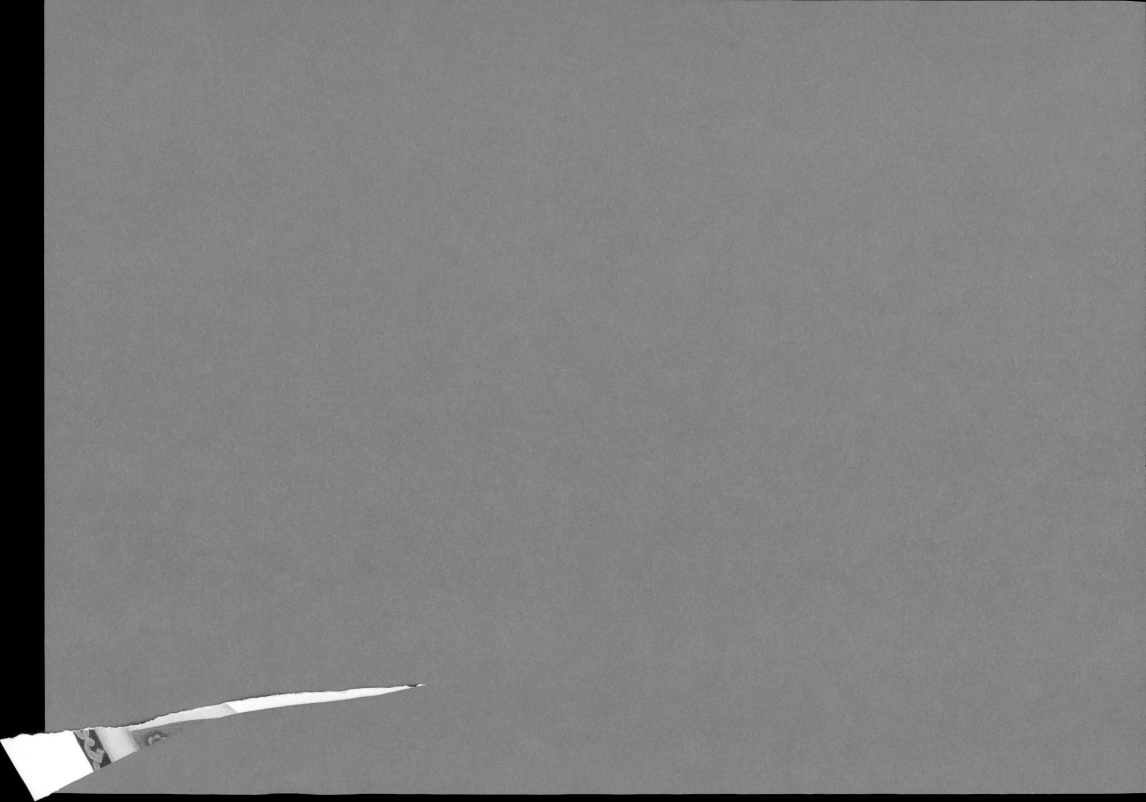

WAY OUT WEST
LIVES A COYOTE
NAMED FRANK

Library of Congress Cataloging-in-Publication Data
Lund, Jillian.
  Way out West lives a coyote named Frank/Jillian Lund.—1st ed.
    p.   cm.
  Summary: Frank the coyote enjoys his desert home and
spending time with his friends and by himself.
  ISBN 0-525-44982-5
  [1. Coyotes—Fiction.   2. Animals—Fiction.   3. West (U.S.)—
Fiction.]   I. Title.
PZ7.L97882Way   1993
[E]—dc20   91-46011   CIP   AC

Published in the United States 1993 by
Dutton Children's Books,
a division of Penguin Books USA Inc.
375 Hudson Street, New York, New York 10014

Designed by Joseph Rutt

Printed in Hong Kong   First edition
10 9 8

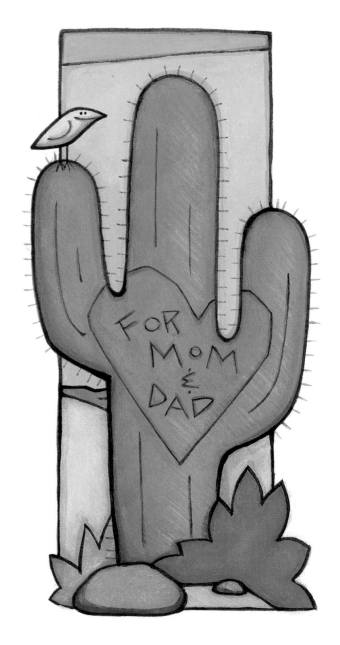

WAY OUT WEST LIVES A COYOTE NAMED FRANK

BY JILLIAN LUND

DUTTON CHILDREN'S BOOKS · NEW YORK

Way out West lives a coyote named Frank.

In the morning Frank likes to watch the sun come up,

and in the evening he likes to watch the sun set.

Frank has a friend named Larry.

Frank and Larry like to chase rabbits

and dig up mouses' houses.

Once they dug up a porcupine's house,
but they never did that again.

Once they chased a skunk,

but they never did that again either!

Frank has another friend.

Her name is Melanie.

Frank and Melanie have a lot in common.

They both like to bother burros

and make trouble for horned toads and Gila monsters.

They both think that scorpions are scary

and that tortoises are tricky.

No one has to tell them to stay far away from rattlesnakes.

Sometimes Frank likes to be by himself.

When Frank is alone, he can catch up on his reading

or take a nap.

He can work on a favorite hobby

or pursue a new interest.

More than anything, Frank likes to get together with all of his

coyote friends to say hello to the moon.
Because that's what coyotes do best way out West.